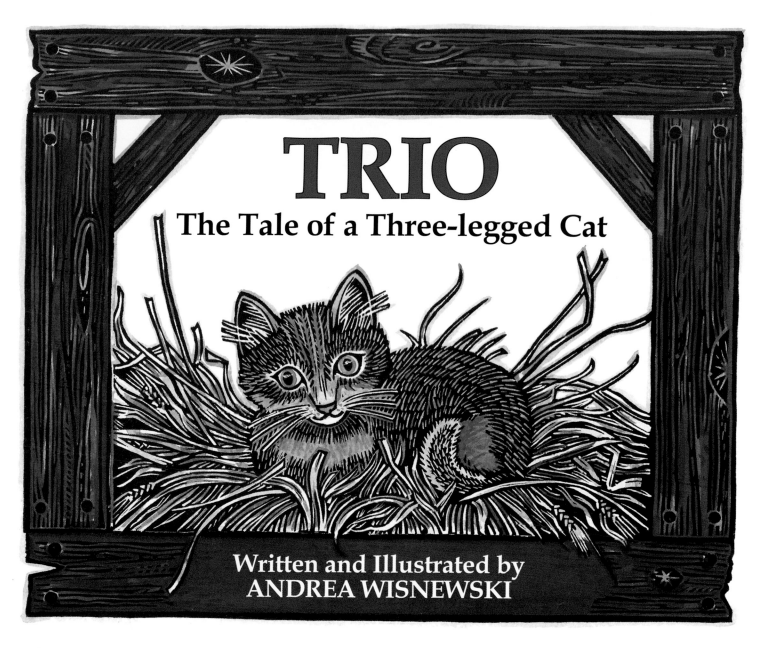

TRIO
The Tale of a Three-legged Cat

Written and Illustrated by
ANDREA WISNEWSKI

David R. Godine, Publisher · *Boston*

First published in 2017 by
David R. Godine · *Publisher*
Post Office Box 450
Jaffrey, New Hampshire 03452
www.godine.com

Library of Congress Cataloging-in-Publication Data

Names: Wisnewski, Andrea, author, illustrator.
Title: Trio : the tale of a three-legged cat / Andrea Wisnewski.
Description: Jaffrey, New Hampshire : David R. Godine - Publisher, 2017. |
Summary: A kitten born with only three legs loves doing the same things as
the chickens who share a garage with him, including sitting on a nest.
Identifiers: LCCN 2017021299 | ISBN 9781567926088 (alk. paper)
Subjects: LCSH: Cats--Juvenile fiction. | CYAC: Cats--Fiction. |
Animals--Infancy--Fiction. | Chickens--Fiction. | Determination
(Personality trait)--Fiction.
Classification: LCC PZ10.3.W6887 Tri 2017 | DDC [E]--dc23
LC record available at https://lccn.loc.gov/2017021299

First edition
Printed in China

For
Anders & Conrad
Trio

One night, in a garage,
in a worn-out old wing chair,
four kittens were born.

One was black,

One was white,

One was striped,

and one was grey, but different.

He only had three legs,
so he was called Trio.

Trio didn't feel different.

He could pounce.

He could sneak.

He could jump, whoops, well sort of!

The kittens shared the garage with eleven chickens.

The chickens didn't altogether approve of the kittens' activities, especially Trio's.

On fine days, the chickens were let out
in the garden to roam.

Trio followed at a safe distance...
chickens could be testy.

Trio liked to do whatever the chickens did.
The chickens dug holes and took dust baths.

So did Trio.

The chickens scratched for bugs and ate them.

So did Trio, yuck!

The chickens did one thing that Trio could not do,
no matter how hard he tried.

One day when the chickens were in the garden,
Trio decided to climb up into the hens' nesting boxes.

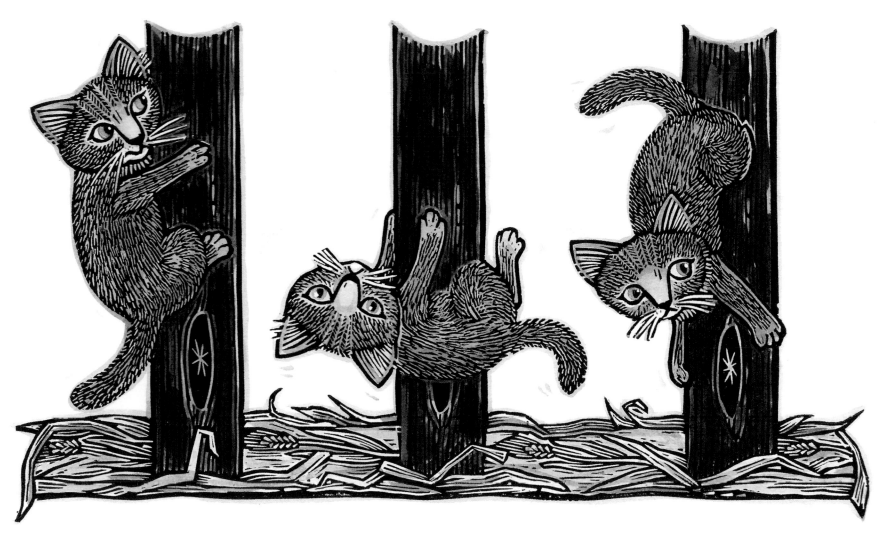

He tried,   and tried,   and tried again.

Trio didn't give up until he found a way…

and finally he did!

Trio came and sat in the nest every day as soon as the chickens left.

It was cozy in there,

and very relaxing.

Then one day in the nest,
Trio felt something strange.

Something was happening…

An egg was hatching! All day, Trio watched the egg.

The other kittens watched the egg.

Even the chickens watched the egg.

Finally, a little chick popped out.

It was the fluffiest, cutest little chick…

with one leg.

Trio thought she was beautiful and named her Uno.

And from that day forward they were always together.

The End

TRIO: The True Story

I FIRST MET TRIO on a snowy day in Minneapolis, Minnesota. I had never seen a three-legged cat before! My husband, Chris, and I were there to help my brother, Anders, and his husband, Conrad, pack for a move to the family farm in Connecticut. Anders told me that a stray cat had her kittens in their garage (which also served as a chicken coop). The mother cat was very wary of anyone coming near her at first, but by feeding her dishes of food, (she was terribly thin!) they earned her trust. When they were allowed closer to the kittens, they noticed a small gray one who was a little different. His left rear leg was missing below the "knee." My brother was upset by this and said, "He only has three legs!" Conrad assured him he would be fine; "He doesn't know that he's any different!" They decided then and there to adopt the kitten that Anders fondly named Trio.

With all the packing—the house; the garage/chicken coop; the eleven chickens; two other cats, Apricot and Snowy; and finally Trio—Anders and Conrad decided they just couldn't keep all the kittens and the mother as well. They found the Southwest Metro Animal Rescue and Adoption Society in Chaska, MN, and brought them there to be adopted by loving families. The move took place in October as the Indian summer lingered. Chris and I were in charge of driving a truck with the eleven chickens in their special traveling crates in the back. Anders and Conrad took all the cats in their kitty carriers in their car. We said goodbye to Minneapolis and drove south-east to Wisconsin, through Illinois and Indiana, stopping twelve hours later at a hotel in Ohio at two in the morning. Anders and Conrad reported that after meowing all day in the car, Trio had slept very soundly in his hotel bed! The next morning we continued through Pennsylvania, New York, and after thirteen hours, we arrived in Connecticut. The chickens were very happy to see their new coop that night!

Trio lives happily on his farm and enjoys doing everything other cats can do. He runs through the fields, climbs the apple trees in the orchard, and carefully spies on the chickens from the tall grass. After a full day, he curls up on a warm lap and falls asleep dreaming of moles.